A Note to Parents and Caregivers:

Read-it! Readers are for children who are just starting on the amazing road to reading. These beautiful books support both the acquisition of reading skills and the love of books.

The RED LEVEL presents familiar topics using common words and repeating sentence patterns.

The BLUE LEVEL presents new ideas using a larger vocabulary and varied sentence structure.

The YELLOW LEVEL presents more challenging ideas, a broad vocabulary, and wide variety in sentence structure.

The GREEN LEVEL presents more complex ideas, an extended vocabulary range, and expanded language structures.

When sharing a book with your child, read in short stretches, pausing often to talk about the pictures. Have your child turn the pages and point to the pictures and familiar words. And be sure to reread favorite stories or parts of stories.

There is no right or wrong way to share books with children. Find time to read with your child, and pass on the legacy of literacy.

Adria F. Klein, Ph.D.
Professor Emeritus
California State University
San Bernardino, California

Managing Editor: Bob Temple
Creative Director: Terri Foley
Editor: Brenda Haugen
Editorial Adviser: Andrea Cascardi
Copy Editor: Laurie Kahn
Designer: Melissa Voda
Page production: The Design Lab
The illustrations in this book were rendered in watercolor, colored pencil, and ink.

Picture Window Books
5115 Excelsior Boulevard
Suite 232
Minneapolis, MN 55416
1-877-845-8392
www.picturewindowbooks.com

Printed in the United States of America.

Library of Congress Cataloging-in-Publication Data
Blair, Eric.
The brave little tailor / by Jacob and Wilhelm Grimm ; adapted by Eric Blair ;
illustrated by David Shaw.
p. cm. — (Read-it! readers fairy tales)
Summary: An easy-to-read retelling of the classic tale of a tailor whose boast about
killing seven flies at one blow leads him to even greater feats.
ISBN 1-4048-0315-7 (Library Binding)
[1. Fairy tales. 2. Folklore—Germany.] I. Grimm, Jacob, 1785-1863. II. Grimm,
Wilhelm, 1786-1859. III. Shaw, David, 1947- ill. IV. Brave little tailor. English.
V. Title. VI. Series.
PZ8.B5688Br 2004
398.2—dc22   2003014038

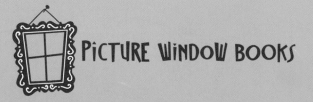

The Brave Little Tailor

A Retelling of the Grimms' Fairy Tale
By Eric Blair

Illustrated by David Shaw

Content Adviser:
Kathy Baxter, M.A.
Former Coordinator of Children's Services
Anoka County (Minnesota) Library

Reading Advisers:
Adria F. Klein, Ph.D.
Professor Emeritus, California State University
San Bernardino, California

Susan Kesselring, M.A.
Literacy Educator
Rosemount-Apple Valley-Eagan (Minnesota) School District

Picture Window Books
Minneapolis, Minnesota

About the Brothers Grimm

To help a friend, brothers Jacob and Wilhelm
Grimm began collecting old stories told
in their home country of Germany. Events
in their lives would take the brothers away
from their project, but they never forgot
about it. Several years later, the Grimms
published their first books of fairy tales.
The stories they collected still are enjoyed
by children and adults today.

Once upon a time, there was a little tailor.
One day, he was sewing at his table.
Flies flew onto his snack of bread and jam.
The little tailor shooed them away
with his hand.

When the flies returned to the bread and jam,
the tailor reached for a dust cloth.
He smacked the flies with the cloth.

After the blow, the tailor counted
seven dead flies. He was pleased
with himself. "The town should know
of this mighty stroke. No, the whole world
should know!" he cried.

The tailor cut out a belt. He sewed letters onto the belt. They spelled *seven at one blow.* He decided his shop was too small for such a brave man. The little tailor packed and left.

On his journey, he met a giant. "I'm off to see the world. Would you like to join me?" asked the tailor. The giant only laughed.

"You are just a crumb," the giant said.

The tailor opened his coat and said,
"That's a good joke. Look at my belt."
The giant saw *seven at one blow.*
He thought the brave tailor had killed
seven men with one blow.

The giant was afraid the tailor might harm him and the other giants. He came up with a plan to get rid of the tailor. "My brothers and I live nearby. Why don't you spend the night in our cave?" asked the giant. The tailor happily agreed.

The giant's bed was too big. The tailor
decided to sleep on the floor. At midnight,
the giant crept in with his walking stick.
He hit the bed so hard, it broke in two.
The giant thought he had killed the tailor.

The next day, the giants went out walking in the woods. They met the cheerful tailor, alive and well. The giants were so surprised and frightened, they ran away.

The tailor followed the road to a palace.
He lay down on the grass and fell asleep.
While he slept, people saw him and
noticed his belt. "Seven at one blow,"
one man said. "He must be a mighty hero.
We should tell the king."

The king wanted such a man for his army.
When the tailor woke up, a messenger
offered him a house and a special
place in the king's army. The tailor
gladly accepted.

The soldiers were jealous. "If you don't get rid of him, we are all leaving," one soldier said to the king. But they were afraid of a man who could kill seven at one blow. They didn't know he was only a tailor.

The king had a plan. "Two evil giants live in the forest," the king told the tailor. "If you kill them, you can marry my daughter and have half my kingdom. You may take 100 soldiers to help you."

"I accept," said the tailor. "That should be easy work for a man who kills seven at one blow. I don't need your soldiers. I shall do it alone."

The tailor went into the forest. The soldiers
followed far behind. The tailor found
the two evil giants sleeping under a tree.
He filled his pockets with stones
and climbed into the tree.

The tailor dropped stones onto the sleeping giants. "Why did you hit me?" one giant asked the other.

"It wasn't me," he said. "You're dreaming." They went back to sleep.

The tailor dropped more stones as
the giants slept. "Stop it!" said one giant.

"I didn't do anything," said the other.
The giants were so angry, they began
to fight.

The giants tore trees from the ground
and beat each other to death. The tailor
climbed down from his tree and stabbed
the giants with his sword. He wanted
to make it look as if he had killed the giants.
Then he went back to the king.

The king refused to give the tailor his reward.
He still wanted to get rid of the tailor.
"Before I give you my daughter and half
my kingdom, you must catch the unicorn
in the forest," the king said.

"Gladly," said the tailor. "That should be easy work for a man who kills seven at one blow." He set off into the woods with a rope and an ax.

Before long, the unicorn passed by.
The tailor was standing in front of a tree.
When the unicorn saw the tailor, he rushed
to spike him with his horn.

At the last moment, the tailor jumped aside.
The unicorn drove his horn into the tree
and was stuck. The tailor put the rope
around the unicorn's neck and cut his
horn free with the ax. The tailor returned
to the king.

The king again refused to give the little tailor his reward. "You must catch the wild boar in the forest," said the king.

"That should be easy work for a man who kills seven at one blow," the tailor said. He went back to the forest.

The boar saw the tailor and chased him.
The tailor ran into a chapel, and the boar
followed. The tailor climbed out a window,
ran around to the door, and slammed
the door shut. The boar could not escape.
He was too big to get out through
the window.

The tailor went to the king to claim
his reward. This time, the king couldn't refuse.
The king's daughter had to marry the tailor.
There was a royal wedding, and the tailor
became a king.

One night, the tailor's wife heard him talking in his sleep. "Patch those pants, lad," said the tailor. She went to report this to her father.

"My husband is only a poor tailor," she said. They decided to send men to kill the tailor in his sleep.

The tailor found out about the plan.
When the men crept to the bedroom door,
the tailor pretended to talk in his sleep.
"I killed seven at one blow and two giants,
captured a unicorn, and caught a wild boar.
Why should I fear the men at the door?"
Frightened, the men ran away, and the tailor
remained king all his life.

Levels for *Read-it!* Readers

**Read-it! Readers help children practice early reading skills
with brightly illustrated stories.**

Red Level: Familiar topics with frequently used words and repeating patterns.

Blue Level: New ideas with a larger vocabulary and a variety of language structures.

Little Red Riding Hood, by Maggie Moore 1-4048-0064-6

The Three Little Pigs, by Maggie Moore 1-4048-0071-9

Yellow Level: Challenging ideas with an expanded vocabulary and a wide variety of sentences.

Cinderella, by Barrie Wade 1-4048-0052-2

Goldilocks and the Three Bears, by Barrie Wade 1-4048-0057-3

Jack and the Beanstalk, by Maggie Moore 1-4048-0059-X

The Three Billy Goats Gruff, by Barrie Wade 1-4048-0070-0

Green Level: More complex ideas with an extended vocabulary range and expanded language structures.

The Brave Little Tailor, by Eric Blair 1-4048-0315-7

The Bremen Town Musicians, by Eric Blair 1-4048-0310-6

The Emperor's New Clothes, by Susan Blackaby 1-4048-0224-X

The Fisherman and His Wife, by Eric Blair 1-4048-0317-3

The Frog Prince, by Eric Blair 1-4048-0313-0

Hansel and Gretel, by Eric Blair 1-4048-0316-5

The Little Mermaid, by Susan Blackaby 1-4048-0221-5

The Princess and the Pea, by Susan Blackaby 1-4048-0223-1

Rumpelstiltskin, by Eric Blair 1-4048-0311-4

The Shoemaker and His Elves, by Eric Blair 1-4048-0314-9

Snow White, by Eric Blair 1-4048-0312-2

The Steadfast Tin Soldier, by Susan Blackaby 1-4048-0226-6

Thumbelina, by Susan Blackaby 1-4048-0225-8

The Ugly Duckling, by Susan Blackaby 1-4048-0222-3